Stitches

By
Kevin Morrison

Illustrations by
John Nixon

Ambassador Books, Inc.
Worcester • Massachusetts

Kevin Morrison can be emailed at: wrytingbear@hotmail.com.

Library of Congress Cataloging-in-Publication Data

Morrison, Kevin, 1973-
  Stitches / by Kevin Morrison ; illustrations by John Nixon.
      p. cm.
Summary: One of the balls in a baseball factory, which dreams of playing in the major leagues, has a happy and surprising life after a mailman takes him home to his young son.
  ISBN 1-929039-15-8
  [1. Self-actualization (Psychology)--Fiction. 2. Baseballs--Fiction. 3. Baseball--Fiction. 4. Fathers and sons--Fiction.] I. Nixon, John, ill.
II. Title.

PZ7.M82965St 2003
[E]--dc21
                                         2002154152

ISBN-13: 978-1-929039-15-9
ISBN-10:   1-929039-15-8

Published in the United States by Ambassador Books, Inc.
91 Prescott Street • Worcester, Massachusetts 01605
(800) 577-0909

For current information about all titles from Ambassador Books, Inc. visit our web-site at: www.ambassadorbooks.com.
Printed in China.

Dedication

To every father who got out his old baseball glove,
To every mother who tried to get the grass stains out,
For every time you said, "You can do it!"
Thank You.

Under every sunrise,

    a new story begins.

Behind every sunset,

    is a dream come true.

It was an especially bright morning in the town of Middlefield. It had rained the day before and all through the night, but the sun rose to a clear sky and sparkled on the dew-covered ground.

A little old man named Doogan was on his way to work. As he walked he whistled, and as he whistled he wobbled from side to side.

Everyone in Middlefield called Doogan "Ducky" because he walked like the ducks down at the lake. He didn't mind. His mother always told him that nicknames were a sign of affection.

Ducky worked at the old Middlefield baseball factory. He had worked there since he was a kid. His first job had been to deliver boxes of new baseballs to local sporting goods stores. Seventy years later, he was still at it.

Ducky was always the first one to arrive at work, and he liked it that way. In the early morning when the factory was calm and quiet, he would sit down with a cup of coffee and talk to Jasper, the stray cat that had made the factory his home.

Ducky had a different job now. He was in charge of taking out the bad or defective baseballs before they were shipped to sporting goods stores near and far.

Everyone in Middlefield loved Ducky— except, of course, the baseballs in the baseball factory. If you didn't pass Ducky's inspection, your dreams of fame and the major leagues were over.

Every morning there was a barrel full of

balls waiting to be inspected. They were brand new with bright white skin and beautiful red stitching. Some were going to be shipped to sporting goods stores, some were headed for Little League teams, and a select few were destined for the major leagues. Some of the balls had heard stories of others making it all the way to the Hall of Fame, where millions of people came to see them every year.

On this morning, one of the balls in the barrel was very nervous. He dreamed of a life in the major leagues, but he knew that his stitching was a little crooked. So the ball tried to sit so his crooked stitches could not be seen, hoping that Ducky would not notice.

All the balls in the barrel got excited when they heard Ducky's footsteps coming.

"Good morning friends," Ducky said. "Who's ready to play today?"

One by one, Ducky picked up the balls. He inspected each one closely, looking for flaws

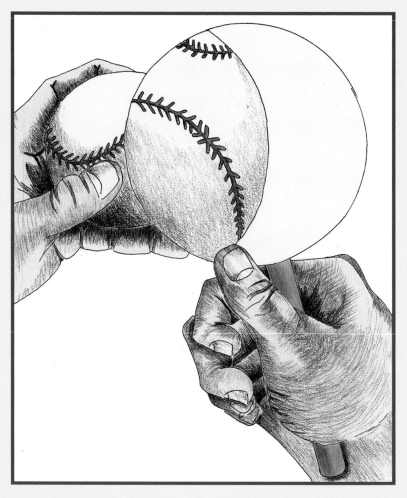

or scuffs. When he found a perfect ball, he put it in a box to be shipped. When he came across one that had a flaw, he tossed it in an old canvas bag on the floor.

With each ball that went before him, the ball

with the crooked stitches grew more nervous. Finally, Ducky picked him up. He rolled the ball around in his hand to check how it felt.

"Hmmm, it feels good. It looks clean."

The ball thought that just maybe he would pass the inspection.

"Oh, wait a minute," Ducky said. "That stitching is just a bit crooked. I almost missed that."

Ducky tossed the ball with the crooked stitches over his shoulder and into the old canvas bag. There were a few balls in there already, and most of them did not want to talk.

The ball with the crooked stitches rolled over to the corner of the bag. He wanted to be alone. He was startled when one of the other balls approached him.

"So, what are you in for? Do you have scuffs? Are you lopsided?"

"My stitching is crooked," the ball answered. He began to cry.

"Now listen up, Stitches," the other ball said sharply. "I won't stand for any crying in this bag. It could be much worse. You could have been a tennis ball or a golf ball. Personally, I'd rather be a defective baseball. Now pull yourself together!"

"Why did you call me 'Stitches'?" the ball asked. "It's not very nice to make fun of others, you know."

"I'm not making fun of you, Stitches. If I called you 'Ball,' everyone in this bag would think I was talking to them. If you want to, you can call me 'Scuffs.' "

"I guess you're right, Scuffs, but what do I have to be happy about?" Stitches asked.

"Well, I don't know yet. You have a special purpose in life. We all do. You just have to be ready for it when it comes."

As Scuffs finished talking, there was a big jolt. Ducky had grabbed the bag and was taking the balls out of the factory.

Ducky whistled a merry tune, as he slung the bag over his shoulder. He carried the balls down the street and around the corner. When he came to a little shop, Ducky pushed the door open. A little bell rang telling the shop-keeper that they were there.

"Hey, John!" Ducky said. "I've got some more baseballs for you."

"Great, Ducky!" the shopkeeper replied. "I'm just about out."

Stitches began to wonder where they were. Before his mind could wander very far, the canvas bag was tipped upside down and all the baseballs tumbled down into an old wooden crate.

"I'll see you next week, John!" Ducky said as he left the shop. And just like that, it was all over. Stitches looked around and saw that he and the other balls were in a box with old beat-up sporting equipment. There was a bent tennis racquet, a flat football, and one boxing glove. They were in a secondhand store, surrounded by other people's discarded stuff.

Stitches could not believe it. In one day's time he had gone from dreams of making it to the major leagues to dreams of getting out of a junk box. Stitches did not like the way the old boxing glove smelled, so he hoped he would get out soon.

A week went by and not one customer looked in the wooden crate. Not many customers came into the shop. It wasn't a busy place like a grocery or department store. Sometimes people would come in and look around. Sometimes people would come in just to chat with the shopkeeper.

For a long time, Stitches would get excited whenever he heard the little bell on the door jingle. But after a while, Stitches didn't get excited anymore. He just knew that nobody was going to buy him.

Then one day the door opened and the little bell jingled. Stitches hardly noticed. It was only the mailman who came in every day. He usually dropped off the mail and hurried away to his next stop. But today he stopped.

The mailman looked over at the box of junk.

"Hey John, I want one of those baseballs to take home to my son. How much?" the mailman asked.

Stitches perked up at the unexpected turn of events.

"Oh, just take one. You don't expect me to charge you for a little baseball do you?" the shopkeeper laughed. "It's on the house."

"Thanks, John! My son will love it!"

The mailman walked over to the box and picked up the baseball next to Stitches.

Stitches wanted to cry again, but he remembered what Scuffs said and held back his tears.

Then to his surprise the mailman dropped the other ball back in the box and picked up Stitches.

Stitches' heart began to race. This might be his chance! The mailman held him in his hand for what seemed a long time.

"This one will do just fine," the mailman said. "Thanks again."

The mailman dropped Stitches in his mailbag and left the shop. Stitches was overjoyed. He knew that he was getting a chance that the other balls in the shop might never get. They each had a special purpose in life, Scuffs had told him. He just had to be ready when his chance came. And Stitches knew he was ready.

When the mailman went home that evening, he found his little boy in the front yard tossing a pine cone up in the air and trying to catch it.

When the little boy saw his father, he dropped the pine cone and ran to him and gave him a big hug.

"Guess what I got for you today, Danny!"

the mailman said. Danny's eyes lit up. The mailman reached into his mailbag and pulled out Stitches.

"Wow!" Danny yelled. "Thanks, Dad!"

"The stitching is a little crooked, but it will work just fine."

At first Stitches was embarrassed that the mailman had pointed out his crooked stitches, but Danny didn't care about the stitching. He loved his new baseball, and the baseball loved Danny. It no longer mattered to Stitches that he was not quite perfect.

"You know, I think I have an old bat in the garage somewhere. I'll teach you how to hit tomorrow."

Danny gave his dad another big hug.

The next evening, and for many evenings after that, Danny and his dad went to the park with Stitches and the old bat. Each time his father pitched the ball, Danny would swing at it with all his might. But he missed it each and every time. No matter how hard he tried, Danny couldn't hit the ball. One evening after a big swing and miss, he sat down on the ground and tears rolled down his cheeks.

"Danny, you can do it," his dad said. "I know you can."

"I'm never going to be a baseball player like those guys on TV," Danny cried.

His dad put his arm around Danny's shoulder and said, "They started out just like you, Danny. They had to learn from scratch. You have plenty of time and I know you'll be great at whatever you do. Let's try it one more time. Just watch the ball and swing a little softer."

Danny wiped the tears from his eyes and got up to try again. His father believed he could do it, so he did, too. The mailman picked up Stitches and stepped back to toss him to Danny.

"Just watch the ball, Danny."

With that, he pitched the ball slowly and right over the rock they were using for home plate. Danny swung the old bat and hit

Stitches high over his dad's head and into the
bushes by the playground.

The mailman threw his arms in the air and
shouted, "YES!! You did it, Danny!"

He picked up his son and held him tight.

"That was a great hit, just like those guys on TV," he said.

Danny smiled and laughed.

"Wait a minute! If you're like those guys on TV, I need to get your autograph!"

The mailman set his son back down and ran to get Stitches out of the bushes. He brought him back and pulled a pen out of his pocket.

"Can I have your autograph, Mister?" he asked Danny.

"Sure!" Danny said. He took Stitches and the pen and signed his name. He handed it back to his biggest fan.

"Thanks, Mister!" his dad said. "You're the greatest!"

From that day on, Danny and his Dad never missed a chance to go to the park and practice.

Stitches got pretty beat up. He was soaked

by the rain, run over by a car, and chewed by a dog. His cover was marked with grass stains and lots of scuffs, but you could still see Danny's name right where he signed it that wonderful day.

As time went by, Danny grew taller and bigger and stronger, and sometimes he hit Stitches so far that he and his dad had trouble finding the ball.

Then one day, Danny left for college. Stitches, along with Danny's toys and other things, was stored in a box and put in a closet.

Sometimes the closet door would open, but no one ever opened the box. Even so, Stitches was happy. He knew that he had fulfilled his purpose, and he would not have chosen any other life than the one he had.

Years and years went by. Stitches lost count after so many.

Then one day, the closet door was opened. The mailman, who was now old and gray and moved very slowly, knelt over the box. When he saw Stitches, a giant grin came across his face.

"There you are!" he said. "You're going to make a special trip!"

Stitches didn't know what the mailman was talking about, but he enjoyed seeing him again. He was carefully wrapped up and placed in another box all by himself.

The retired mailman took him down to the post office and sent him on his way. Stitches was sad to leave, but he knew it must be for the best.

A few days later, the box was opened again. This time, Stitches didn't see a familiar face. It was another old man, but he seemed very excited as he reached in to pick up Stitches.

"Oh, my! This is quite a ball," he said. "Everybody is going to love you!"

The old man carried Stitches down a hallway to a big glass case. He opened the case and set Stitches inside.

Stitches couldn't believe it! In the back of the case was a picture of Danny!

The old man closed the glass case and stood back to look at the display. Before he turned to walk away, he said something that Stitches never thought he would hear.

"Welcome to the Hall of Fame."

Stitches could not believe what he heard. There was another ball in the case next to Stitches. He was much newer and had hardly been used at all.

"Excuse me," Stitches said. "Did he just say, 'Welcome to the Hall of Fame'?"

"Yes sir, he did, and I have to say that I am truly honored to meet you!"

Stitches was a little confused. He didn't understand how anybody—especially a ball in the Hall of Fame—could be honored to meet him, the defective ball from the old Middlefield baseball factory.

"Without you, I wouldn't be here," the other ball said.

"I don't understand. What do you mean?" Stitches asked.

The other ball paused and then began to tell Stitches about Danny and how he had made it to the major leagues. Stitches listened with excitement to every word.

"I am Danny's 756th home run. He hit more than anybody who ever played the game. But he wouldn't have hit any if it hadn't been for you."

The two baseballs talked all night long sharing stories and laughing. They became the best of friends. The next morning and every morning after, the Hall of Fame opened and people came in to look at them. Stitches thought about his life and how he had gone from the old canvas bag to a glass case at the Hall of Fame. It was an amazing story.

One day, years later, Danny came in to the Hall of Fame. He was old and gray now, and he looked a lot like the mailman when he pulled Stitches out of the closet. Danny walked up to the glass case and knelt down to get a closer look at the grass-stained ball he had signed so long ago. He put his hand on the glass by Stitches and smiled.

"Thank you, old friend."

31

Under every sunrise,
    a new story begins.

Behind every sunset,
    is a dream come true.

In our lives, as in the life of Stitches, it doesn't matter who we are, where we come from, or where we live. It only matters whose name is signed on our hearts.

God lovingly autographed each one of us before we were even born. You don't have to play in the major leagues to make God's Hall of Fame. It only matters how you use the talents and the life that God gave you.